My Old Gray Coat

Mountainhome Musing

Joe Shannon

2007

Parkway Publishers, Inc.
Boone, North Carolina

2007
Published by Parkway Publishers, Inc.
Box 3678
Boone, North Carolina
www.parkwaypublishers.com

Joe Shannon lives in Boone, North Carolina.
He is a teacher, musician, and concert host.

For information about his concert series,
Mountainhome Music,
go to *www.mountainhomemusic.com.*

Library of Congress Cataloging-in-Publication Data

Shannon, Joe Wayne, 1949-
  My old gray coat : Mountainhome musing / Joe Shannon.
    p. cm.
  ISBN-13: 978-1-933251-39-4
  1. Shannon, Joe W.--Anecdotes. I. Title.
  ML419.S423A3 2006
  781.642092--dc22
  [B]

                                    2006021008

Editor/Book Designer: Julie L. Shissler
Cover Design: Aaron Burleson

Preface

I didn't plan to write this book. It evolved. As a performing musician, I learned that sharing a thought, a poem, a story helped to accentuate the mood of my music. As a concert host, I expanded my use of the written word to complement the music of others. One concert, two; one year, two years, five years, ten—the collection grew. Themes emerged. A book was born: My Old Gray Coat. I hope it fits.

Joe Shannon

Table of Contents

Perhaps They Heard

Blue Ridge Blue & Gray

Eternal Moments

I Am a Pilgrim

School Days

Teacher Days

Short Tales

I Am

Country Roads Less Traveled

Thanks to

Amy Hiatt, Kim Bentley,
and Jeannie Jernigan
for previewing
this manuscript

Perhaps They Heard

Something About Freedom

I know something about freedom, but there is much more I don't know. I don't know freedom as well as the Jews who were liberated by the allies at Auschwitz, Dachau, and Treblinka. I don't know freedom as well as Rosa Parks, who stood against the social tide by refusing to move to the back of the bus. I don't know the desire for freedom nearly as well as the unnamed young man who faced down a column of Red Army tanks on their way to Tienamin Square.

I don't know the origins of freedom, the essential desire for human dignity, as well as Mother Teresa who helped the dying and dispossessed in the squalid streets of Calcutta, and not as well as Albert Schweitzer, who used his genius in medicine and music to serve the needy in remote places rather than the advantaged in places of privilege.

I don't know the price of freedom nearly as well as the soldiers who pushed Germany back within its borders in WWI; who faced Kamikaze pilots in the Pacific and defeated fascism in Europe in WWII; who served—and continue to serve—as a human buffer between North and South Korea; who stood against communism in Vietnam; and who once again stand between those who cannot or will not respect human rights and human differences in places all around the world. I don't know the price of freedom as well as children orphaned by war, not as well as widowed spouses, and not as well as Gold Star mothers.

I *do know* that the cause of freedom can be, has been, and is advanced in many different ways. It is advanced by soldiers and civil servants who keep the peace, by entrepreneurs who create opportunity, by clergy who minister, doctors who heal, teachers who inform, artists who inspire, and by an infinite number of silent Samaritans who weave a moral fabric of caring and compassion that binds us into community and country.

To the giants of moral courage—to soldiers, civil servants, and Samaritans—to all who have given, and are giving, the breath of life to the body of freedom, much is owed, very much. This I know for sure. This I know.

2001

Perhaps They Heard

A Memorial Day Salute

About ten years ago I was on my way to Harrisburg, Pennsylvania to play for a wedding. Until I noticed the monuments and tombstones, I didn't realize that my route took me through the heart of the Gettysburg Battlefield. It was dusk, late in the fall; the trees were bare, the air cold and gray, and the park was empty. I had a little extra time, so I decided to look around—to imagine the sights and sounds and to feel the significance of this historic place.

Narrow roads and split rail fences separated the present from the past and the secular from the sacred. As if walking, I drove slowly through the rolling hills: past where Picket charged and where McPherson farmed, past waves of white tombstones and autumn leaves at rest, and past my ability to measure and to comprehend.

To get a broader perspective, I got out of my car and walked up the gray-stone stairs of a marble edifice that was inlaid with canon, sword, and rifle—and with faces forever fearful. At the highest place on which I could stand, I put my harmonica to my lips and slowly played *Dixie*. Then I faced the opposite direction and played the *Battle Hymn of the Republic*. My music became my prayer: for the fallen, for myself, and for all that is healing and hopeful and good. As far as I know, no one saw or heard.

If anyone did hear, perhaps they also heard at Andersonville and Arlington and on the Arizona. Perhaps they heard at Normandy, in the Philippines, and in Panama. Perhaps they heard in Korea, Vietnam, Beirut and Bosnia, and in Iran and Iraq. Perhaps they heard in Greensboro and

Salisbury and at St. John's Church on a hilltop in the valley of the cross. Perhaps they heard just up the road and across the way.

But as far as I know, no one saw or heard. As far as I know....

2003

Blue Ridge Blue and Gray

Background

Blue Ridge Blue & Gray *is a play about the Civil War in the mountains of western North Carolina. Written as historical fiction, it was first performed at Farthing Auditorium at Appalachian State University on December 3, 1998. "Banjo Betsy," "Slaughter at Shelton Laurel," "My Old Gray Coat," and "I'm Coming Home" are excerpts from* Blue Ridge Blue & Gray.

Banjo Betsy

Jacob, a middle aged man, is wrestling with his conflicted feelings about the war. The war is still young, but he has already experienced the horrors of battle. The scene begins with Jacob playing "Home Sweet Home" on the banjo. After he stops to share his thoughts, his banjo "sings" to keep him company. "Banjo Betsy" is representative of Confederate mountaineers' motivation to fight.

Betsy and I spend a lot of time together. I like having my arms around her.

I like to touch her skin and run my fingers along her long, slender neck. And when she speaks, boy, it's music to my ears. To tell you the truth, old Betsy here's the best banjo I've ever had.

My daughter said I was too old to be off fighting. I think she understood me leaving; but not leaving to fight. Her young age, yes, but there's also a division between her mother and I. I believe I'm doing the right thing. Her mother, a Quaker, does not share in this belief. And about my age, well, I can lift a rifle and pull the trigger just as well as any younger man.

For me, this war is not about slavery. It is about keeping the Yanks from invading my mountains; it is about loyalty to my neighbors; it is about deciding what's best for ourselves—and not somebody else deciding for us.

That's why I'm here. But I hate it. I do not rejoice in victory, and I feel defeat as deeply as any man. If I didn't have the letters from Lorena, if I didn't have the few friends I've made, and if I didn't have old Betsy here to touch, to hold, to play, I think I might give up. Yep, I think I might. Sing to me gal; sing to me.

1996

9

Slaughter at Shelton Laurel

The true story of "The Slaughter at Shelton Laurel" is told through a fictional newspaper story. Although most mountaineers who fought in the Civil War fought for the Confederacy, there was also a strong presence of Unionist sympathizers.

Shelton Laurel is in Madison County, North Carolina, about an hour from Asheville.

Asheville Spectator
February 18, 1863

There was a slaughter of Unionist sympathizers in the Shelton Laurel community of Madison County. It was mostly about grudges—and about salt. As readers know, salt keeps meat from spoiling, and without salt, folks may be left without meat during the long, hard months of winter.

In the Shelton Laurel community, which is a pro-union enclave and very isolated, folks apparently were starving. In the nearby town of Marshall the Confederates maintained a storage bin of salt. Motivated by the need to feed themselves and their children, some Shelton Laurel residents, about fifty, raided this facility. How much salt was taken is not known. Before leaving, the group also raided some homes of prominent Confederate citizens. And, as expected, the Confederate troops retaliated.

The Shelton Laurel men-folk anticipated the retaliation and hid out in the mountains, thinking their women and children would be left alone in their homes. They were wrong. When the Confederate troops arrived, led by Colonel Lawrence Allen, they asked the whereabouts of the men-folk. The women and children would not say.

To try to get them to talk, many of the women and children were hung by the neck, and just before death they were lowered to the ground. This was repeated over and over again. This torture yielded fifteen men-folk that the Confederates found hiding out in the mountains. These men were tied like hogs awaiting slaughter. Two men managed to escape. Thirteen were left.

It was said that Joe Woods, a sixty year-old grand-father, cried out, "For God's sake, men, you're not going to shoot us?" When answered by silence, he begged, "at least give us time to pray." Request denied.

All suffered the same fate—red blood on white ice and snow. This blood affects us all, both Union and Confederate. These were innocent human beings that just wanted to feed their families. The stain on the ground will melt and wash away, but the stain on our memories will remain for generations to come.

1996

My Old Gray Coat

"My Old Gray Coat" reflects the sentimentality of the era. If Jacob doesn't make it home, he wants to be remembered and he wants his wife to be taken care of.

December 8, 1864

Webster County, Virginia

Dear Lorena,
      The Shenandoah Valley is covered with snow,
         covered with campfires,
      and covered with soldiers longing for home.
         Tomorrow the battle will be engaged,
      but tonight I hold malice for none.
         Tonight 'tis you I long to hold;
      tomorrow I hold my gun.
          Lorena, a full moon shines tonight,
         and shadows dance across the snow.
      Willow trees weep, while soldiers sleep,
         winds of fear and loneliness blow.
      Perhaps next spring...well,
         I pray this war will soon be over.
      Do you still wear my old gray coat?
         I can see it wrapped around your shoulders.
      If you do, please take it
         and wrap the arms around you tight
         and know that if I could, I'd be with you
         in your arms tonight.
      When morning comes and I must go,
         When soldiers scream and....
      Well, if per chance we miss next spring,
         just hang my coat on a nail.

Hang it by the door
where you will pass to ages old,
   and Lorena, please remember,
   that old coat that hangs there,
   it will keep you from the cold.

                        Jacob

                        1996

I'm Coming Home

"I'm Coming Home," alludes to the true story of Grant's attempt to begin to heal our nation's divide by showing respect to Lee's defeated army.

Jacob was seriously wounded in the leg near the end of the war. He is crippled. Expecting humiliation by Grant's Army, he is deeply moved by their respect.

April 9ᵗʰ, 1965

Dear Lorena,

I have some good news. I'm coming home. Me and some fellas from over in Tennessee are headed home. I didn't write sooner because I couldn't. A surgeon had me confined to a cot for over a month after cutting some Yankee lead from my left leg. But my strength returns with each step towards home.

We are camped three days south of Appomattox, Virginia. I was there when it ended. It was not what I expected.

We all knew it was over. I thought that for a long time, but some things you just couldn't say out loud.

We were prepared to surrender; we were prepared to give up our mounts and our guns. But Grant said that we might need our horses to plow and our guns to hunt. And he commanded his troops to share with us their rations.

Our faces remained stone and our pride unyielding. But some soldiers took their food, and I'm glad they did. They were starving. As our Army dispersed, Grant had the

Yanks stand at attention—and they saluted us as we passed and headed home. Still in pain and still very full of southern pride, I feigned to take no notice. But I did notice, and as I passed before the Yanks in their formation, I walked as tall, I walked as proud, and I walked as straight as I was able. I did my best to be a good soldier.

Like I said, it's clear and quiet tonight. The air is cool, the fire is warm, and stars fill the sky. I don't know why, but in a way, in an unexpected way, it feels a lot like Christmas. I'll be home soon.

Jacob

1996

Eternal Moments

Mother Ireland

Billowing sails wave on a colorless creaking ship.
Belts loosened by hunger, cracks hunger's painful whip.
Taut and ashy flesh is squeezed tightly to the bone.
Wide and weathered eyes gaze one more time toward home.

For four hundred years, they have crossed this troubled sea.
"I'll be home again," their song, their prayer, their plea.
A small thatched cottage stands empty on the shore.
The lights that once burned there, burn there no more.

All alone she waits, while misty raindrops fall.
Tears roll down her stone gray cheeks, the cliffs of Donegal.
Her womb is black and blighted; her mother's milk is dry.
Seagulls sail like sleepy dreams, from salty lips she sighs.

2000

St. Patrick
March 17, 2006

A citizen-child of Rome's cracking empire,
    who returned to his place of bondage,
    to the lush green fields of Ireland,
    where he had been slave and shepherd,
    where he learned to suffer and to pray.
A priest among druids,
    he merged the Celtic circle and the Christian cross,
    and turned scattered and weathered stones
    into timeless monasteries and places of worship.
He was or he became timeless.

He was with Buddha under the enlightened tree,
    with Gandhi on his peaceful pilgrimage,
    and with Martin Luther King on his journey
        to the mountaintop.
He helped to bury the dead in the death camps
    and was by John Paul's side when he died.
He offered calm after Katrina,
    and helped to light the Olympic flame.

He gives music to O'Carolan's harp and Yeats' verse,
    to Galway's flute, Bernstein's mind,
    Yo-yo's cello, and Doc's guitar.

We celebrate his day of passing and his eternal presence.
He was a saint before there was earthly recognition.
Centuries later he was so ordained,
And today he is so honored.

St. Patrick's Celebration

If I didn't play Irish music and help to put on concerts, most likely, I would give very little thought to St. Patrick's Day. I don't recall ever intentionally wearing green when I was a kid, and I never got pinched. I do recall thinking that derby hats were cool, that dancing leprechauns looked funny, and that after St. Patrick's Day it would soon be warm enough to go swimming.

In high school I began to figure out that St. Patrick's Day was a real day that symbolized something, but I didn't know what and didn't care. History was nothing more than a heavy book I had to carry. St. Patrick's Day wasn't even a holiday. Ireland wasn't in my neighborhood, and my music was old hymns and early rock and roll.

St. Patrick's Day began to become something when I learned that my paternal great grandfather left Ireland during the potato famine and planted his roots in South Georgia. It began to become something when I first heard Cecil Gurganus play old-time fiddle in the Apple Barn in Valle Crucis, when Dave Gaston played "Danny Boy" on the flute, when the gentle hands of Jacquelyn Bartlett plucked her magic harp, and when I first blended these sounds with my own music.

Absent music, perhaps St. Patrick's Day would be nothing more than an opportunity to drink green beer, eat corned beef and cabbage, and wipe my mouth with shamrock napkins. But music is Ireland's heartbeat - and mine. It's a late-in-life discovery that began centuries ago.

Eternal Moments

Thanksgiving is between Halloween and Christmas. Christmas day is between presents and a Holy Presence. We live our lives between birth and death. We snack between meals. We succeed and fail between our fears and our aspirations. We travel between destinations. Is every moment and every place just a pause between another moment and another place? Do we ever arrive? For all of us, death is a final destination; yet, even at this moment, most of us believe that this, too, is but a moment of passage.

Thank goodness for moments of passage, for islands in the oceans, rest stops on the highway, sleep between our days and nights, and sanctuary between our rushing to and fro. Thank goodness for children's play and pervasive hope, for connections between old friends, for a dog at your knee or a cat in your lap, for autumn leaves and sweet red roses; for warm fires and wispy voices; for sunsets and soft new snow, for the memory of loved ones who have crossed the great divide, and for strangers who are momentarily joined by music.

For these eternal moments, thank goodness.

2004

A Fountain of Blessing

Hands. I see my great-grandmother's hands piecing together old cloth to make a new quilt. She softly rocks in a dark, coal-fire lit room, skillfully pushing and pulling and planning and piecing; bringing into one, cloth of different shapes, colors, patterns, and textures. It's been thirty-seven years since Nini's death but her spirit is woven into my memory—and last night, tonight, and tomorrow night—one of her quilts still keeps me warm.

> It's granddaddy's shirt, granny's apron,
> mama's skirt, and daddy's cap.
> It's stripes, plain, and poke-a-dots,
> flowers, bees, and trains,
> flannel, silk, and cotton,
> and an old grease stain.
> A piece of the past,
> a family refrain.
> I am stripes, plain, and poke-a-dots,
> flowers, bees, and trains,
> flannel, silk, and cotton,
> and an old grease stain.
> I'm a piece of all who've gone before.
> I am a cloth of many names.

My own hands are tired from picking up pecans in the yard at my Granny Shannon's house. I know if I pick up enough, the result will be some divinity and some pecan pie. When my sack is full and when I get tired, I go inside and decide to take a nap on the couch. Knowing I love to listen to old hymns, Granny Shannon begins to pass her thin, fragile hands across an old pump organ. I hear one of my favorites, "Come Thou Fount Of Every Blessing."

The living room is warm; thin white curtains frame the windows and the bare pecan trees in the yard. The pedals of the organ steadily whisper and sing, whisper and sing, whisper and sing...

My pillow is laced with embroidered flowers that feel soft against my cheek. Sleep comes easy when I'm covered with a blanket of song. When I awake, flowers are imprinted on my cheek and a song is remembered.

Old quilts, old hymns, loving hands—a tapestry of the past in the present. The spirit is alive and a fountain of blessing has come.

1987

A Place Safe and Warm

Her door was always open
The hinges creaked with time
Her furniture, worn and ragged
She counted pennies and dimes
In a place that was safe and warm

I could rest at granny's house
And dream of things to come
I was a knight in shining armor
A song waiting to be sung
In a place that was safe and warm

Turnip greens were boiling
Baked apples filled the air
The table covered with white linen
Set with dignity and care
In a place that was safe and warm

The call came to me in college
That her door will swing no more
Now she sits at a family table
With those who have gone before
In a place that is safe and warm

2005

Greensleeves

Thou harvest queen and queen of innocence,
Oh, Greensleeves,
Why do you not respond?
I love you deeply.
You smile so sweetly.
I offer you kerchiefs for your lovely head
And a smock that's gold and crimson red.
You're a beautiful woman, a little girl,
Once a grain of sand, now a pearl.
Love must seem so simple to you,
But it turns me in a thousand ways.
You're as deep as Loch Lomond
And as gentle as its waves.
I will wait until fall turns to winter
And winter into spring.
I will wait, Greensleeves,
Until it's harvest time again.

1989

A Full Moon on Freshly Fallen Snow

A wide soft blue light gently rises up from nature's
   snowy blanket

and melts into the darkness of a star-filled sky.

Stillness envelops the night, and reverence settles as
   natural as falling snow.

I hear no sound except that of inspiration.

Peaceful Reminders

The bells are peaceful reminders.
The church is still there, and people still care.
It's time to start school, or its simply time.
Chimes ring out when a baby is born,
And when someone dies,
And it's time to mourn.
The bells are peaceful reminders.

Tonight the bells ring in celebration:
For the snowfall and the night,
For warm fires and beautiful sights,
And for friends who are always there.
Lest I forget these markers of time,
Or simple beauty to find.
The bells are peaceful reminders.

Christmas Candy

I have never been to Cleveland, but I used to love the Cleveland Browns. They had a good football team and good players. They had Jim Brown to run the ball and Lou Groza to kick it. And they wore beautiful brown and orange uniforms that looked good in the mud and snow. They were great, and I saw them play almost every Sunday on TV. Howard Ginn was great too. He lived across the street and kicked for the high school team. Sometimes his name was in the newspaper for kicking field goals and extra points. I wanted my name in the newspaper, and I wanted to be famous like Howard Ginn and Lou Groza and the Cleveland Browns.

I felt famous sometimes when playing football in my yard. Whenever I made a good run or got my shirt ripped or got muddy or bloody or bruised, I was almost like Jim Brown.

One day while I was playing, my mother called me in to take a bath. We were playing "kill-the-man-with-the-ball" in the back yard, and I didn't want to stop. I also didn't look forward to following my brother and sister to the bathtub and sitting in their second-hand water. But I did as told. I might not have been so willing if my mother hadn't told me that my grandfather wanted to take me Christmas shopping. That changed things, so the second-hand, soapy water wasn't that bad.

My grandfather was an engineer for the Southern Railroad. His train was bigger and more powerful than the Cleveland Browns. He also carried peanut butter logs in his pockets, which football players couldn't do. He had silver-white Santa Claus hair, red cheeks, and a big warm smile. Since he was old, though, he sometimes seemed far away, even when he was close by.

The store was covered with smiling Santas, plastic peppermint sticks, snowflakes, and Christmas songs that made me want to slide across the floor. I knew where I wanted to go, so I led the way around the slow adults and shopping carts and store-clerk referees as I ran toward my goal.

I wove by toy trucks and road graders, puzzles and game boards, pogo sticks and tetherballs, and bats and gloves until I came to two football helmets about middle ways up on the shelf. Almost like magic, there were two Cleveland Browns football helmets sitting side by side, both autographed by Lou Groza. They were exactly alike, except one had a facemask on the front and one did not. The one with a facemask looked strong and tough. The one without, looked sort of old-fashioned. When Granddaddy caught up, he asked me if I saw something I liked. "Yes, sir," I said.

"Which one do you like the most?"

I pointed to the plain one, the one without a facemask, because I was afraid that if I pointed to the one I really wanted—I wouldn't get it. It looked expensive, and I knew not to ask for expensive things. My mother told me that. And if something was too expensive, well I knew that not even Santa would leave it in our living room. So I asked for what I didn't want, hoping I would get what I wanted.

When Christmas night finally came, I decided I would try to stay awake so I could hear Santa when he came; it didn't work. After I said good night, the next thing I remember was, "Get up, Santa Claus has come." I jumped out of bed and ran to the living room. I saw a pogo stick, a bat and a glove, and some big boxes on the couch. I bounced on the pogo stick, made sure the glove fit, and ran my hands up and down the shiny new Louisville Slugger. After my brother and sister discovered their Christmas toys, we sat in a circle and Daddy passed out our presents. Ann got a pair of skates, Lee got a boat paddle, Mama got a toaster, Daddy got a drill, MaMa got some potholders, Granddaddy got a flashlight, and then finally it was my turn. My present was covered with thin white paper and wrapped with silver and blue ribbon. I quickly broke the ribbon and pulled the paper off the box, but it was taped and hard to open. Mama went to the kitchen to get a pair of scissors. It seemed like she was gone forever. Ann was trying on her skates, Lee was pretending to paddle a boat, and our cat, Tink, was playing with the paper underneath the Christmas tree. Finally Mama returned with the scissors. As I pulled my football helmet out of the box, I saw that it was the one I asked for— and hoped I wouldn't get.

Mama said, "Didn't we have a wonderful Christmas? Santa Claus sure was good to us this year." Then she told us to get out of our pajamas and into our clothes, since it would soon be time for breakfast.

I took my stuff back to my room, but I didn't change clothes and I wasn't hungry. I got in bed with my helmet and crawled deep beneath my quilts, and I thought and thought and thought. I thought about what my friends might say. Would they make fun of me? Would they say I looked old-fashioned? How could I be famous now? Why didn't granddaddy know what I wanted? Why didn't he know? He was supposed to know!

I wondered if everybody was eating breakfast by now. I crawled to the very bottom of my bed and hid deep beneath my quilt. And even though I didn't want anybody to know where I was, I hoped they missed me. For a moment I felt like somebody was in my room, so I peeked between the stitches in my quilt to see if somebody was there. I didn't see anybody, and soon I fell asleep hugging my Cleveland Browns football helmet.

We had a service at church on Christmas morning. I loved seeing my church friends and singing "Silent Night" and smelling the cinnamon candles and walking on the soft red carpet and watching the candlelight play on the ceiling. The whole church was pretty. On the end of each pew, there was a red bow taped to a piece of Christmas tree limb, on the front of the baptizing pool there was a wreath made of red straw and little silver-tipped pine cones, and behind where the preacher stands there was a big sign that said "Give to the Lottie Moon Christmas Offering." The preacher said Lottie Moon was a missionary who went to tell other people about God. The way he talked, he made her seem very important. It made me wonder if *she* drove trains and carried peanut butter logs in *her* pockets.

While we were singing, I sat next to Granddaddy and I noticed wrinkles in his hands and that his fingers were bent crooked at the ends. I wished they weren't that way, but he could still drive a train and drink coffee and grow roses and turn the pages of the hymnbook.

During church, I sang and prayed when I was supposed to, but it wasn't easy. I was tired and excited and worried and grateful and happy and sad—and it was very hard to keep my mind on the manger. Granddaddy reached out and put his hand on my leg; that was his way of telling me to sit still. And I did. But when he moved his hand, guess what? He left a peanut butter log right there on my leg. It was real quiet in the church and when I started to pull the paper off my peanut butter log, Mrs. Adams turned around and gave me a very mean look. And then granddaddy put his hand on my leg again, and he whispered, "Wait until church is over."

"Yes sir," I said. But I wondered if he and Mrs. Adams knew how hard it was to look at a half open peanut butter log and not eat it.

As much as I loved singing, I couldn't wait for church to get out. Finally the preacher said, "What a wonderful day the Lord has made, and now let us leave with a word of thanks." He asked granddaddy to lead the closing prayer. Now that was something, so I bowed my head and prayed as hard as I could—but I was waiting hard on Amen, too. And when he finally got there, well, I hurried outside the church to eat my peanut butter log. It sure was good.

After we had our big Christmas meal, I went outside to share my treasures and to play football with my friends. I wore my helmet. No one made fun of me, at least as far as I know, and I made some good runs and good catches and good tackles, too. A few weeks later I discovered a plastic facemask sitting on the piano bench in the living room: no note, no tag, no card. It was just sitting there when I came in from school. I took it to my room and screwed it on, and soon after that, like often happens with presents, I used my helmet less and less and less, and eventually it found a home in the back of a closet, until one day, one year, many years ago, it just disappeared.

But my memory of that Christmas long ago remains: of getting what I asked for, of disappointment and relief, of song and season and friends. But mostly I remember my grandfather, his silver-white hair and rosy red cheeks, his quiet and gentle ways. With the wisdom of Saint Nick, he gave me something better than a football helmet, something better than a facemask, something even better than a peanut-butter log. He gave me time, attention, and love—the best gift of all.

In addition to being an engineer, my grandfather made many children happy as Santa Claus in his hometown of Valdosta, Georgia.

I Am a Pilgrim

Suwannee River Snakes

Unlike Stephen Foster, I've been to the Suwannee River, I've been on the Suwannee River and I've been in the Suwannee River. Mossy oak trees line the banks as the snaking dark tonic water runs from the Okefenokee Swamp, through South Georgia and the panhandle of Florida and into the Gulf of Mexico.

As a boy, I used to cross the Suwannee River going to and from my grandparent's house in Valdosta, Georgia. For some reason it was an indicator of extremes. It was either too low or too high or wondrously way beyond its banks. It was a thermometer of excitement as seen from the back seat of our 1957 Chevy station wagon.

As a young man right out of college, I had the experience of spending four weeks in a canoe on the Suwannee with nine other aspiring adults. It was part of my training to be a camp counselor at a year round wilderness camp for children with behavior problems. I was expected to be a model of excellence, morality, and discipline. I did not live up to these expectations.

On about our third week out, sometime during the late afternoon we paddled into one of the many crystal clear springs that feed the Suwannee. As we entered the welcoming water, we came upon five or six coeds, most likely from the nearby University of Florida, swimming and drinking beer. Their bodies were in the water and their bathing suits were on the dock. As expected, the paddles of the ten young men slowed to a crawl; we were sternly directed by our leaders to speed up and to aim our canoe's toward the nearest out-of-sight bend. It was, I thought, impolite not to appreciate this gift. More than that, it was an injustice to deny us this brief connection to the natural world. I don't recall the details now, but somehow, as we

37

paddled by these mermaids, I managed to communicate my desire for a beer. As we turned the bend, we were the recipients of waves and smiles and giggles. Like water running downstream, soon we were gone and they were gone.

The next morning I got up just before the sun and silently made my way to the dock. And there floating beneath the crime scene, tethered to a kite string, was a shiny, bobbing can of Pabst Blue Ribbon. That may have been the best breakfast beer I've ever had. And no one knew, until now.

Once I passed my training and I had been given my station, I managed to get ten adolescent boys into three canoes, and I got back on the Suwannee. One boy, anxious to demonstrate his strength, pushed my canoe off the bank prematurely. And for a moment, I was the only one in the canoe. Quiet innocently, I think, he pushed me into a low hanging branch and into a face-to-face encounter with a more than mature water moccasin. The dangling moccasin dropped into the canoe, and I quickly jumped out. We both survived. I didn't get mad at the boy, but he thought I should have. Thoughtful as I am, I let him paddle my canoe for two days. And he was glad to do it.

Just down river we camped at a place that had more snakes on one piece of land than a porcupine has quills. But, as far as I knew, it was the only non-swamp land we had available to us before nightfall. Once the rowdy boys began to roam, the snakes disappeared, except one.

Fortunately, I was the first one to come upon this bigger-than-your arm rattlesnake. When I yelled for the boys to stay away, they quickly formed a circle around that angry snake. Once cornered, it coiled; the rattles tuned louder, sharper, quicker. I yelled for someone to bring me a boat paddle. I swung, and like a bolt of lightning, the snake struck. I swung, and it struck again and again and again and again and again. The paddle prevailed and slowly the bloody snake loosened its coil and turned belly-up on the ground.

Looking back on it, I don't know why I didn't just walk away, and I don't know why I didn't tell the boys to do the same. If I had, most likely, the snake would have crawled safely into hiding.

I don't know why I didn't think of that then. Maybe curiosity got the best of us all. Maybe so, because I have to say, except for all the bones, it did taste a lot like fried chicken.

2005

Moving to the Mountains

I remember a time when I thought I might be the only one who noticed the beauty of the fall leaves. I thought about telling others, but then I decided to keep it to myself.

I moved to North Carolina from Florida in 1976, first to Hendersonville and two years later to Boone. Contrary to popular perception, North Florida does have four seasons, including a beautiful fall. But it doesn't have the panorama and the spectacle of colors that we have in this place and all across the Blue Ridge Mountains.

My first fall in North Carolina I remember riding the waves around Asheville, sailing on the ocean of green and brown, red and orange, and yellow and gold.

My excursions were relatively solitary. It seemed that every back road was a private, personal discovery, known only to the explorer and to local residents. It seemed and felt private, so I guess it was.

As I became less a newcomer and more of a local, I paid more attention to the crowded highways, hotels and restaurants. I understood that many people seek the high road, the overlook, the mountain peak, hoping to find the unique gift of season, place, and time.

Even stressful traffic jams, even packed shopping aisles, even sharp winds and heavy fogs don't seem to affect this annual autumn pilgrimage. It isn't secret, but it is solitary. And sacred.

2002

Grandfather Mountain

An old man sleeps eternally alone
Resting peacefully on his bed of stone
The trees are his beard, and the wind is his comb
    I see Grandfather Mountain

Down in a meadow called McRae
A fiddler saws ole *Scotland the Brave*
A haunting melody from olden days
    From old Grandfather Mountain

The music reaches to ages yore
From pipes and kilts to Scotland's shore
From across the valley and down the moor
    I hear music on the mountain

An old man sleeps eternally alone
Resting peacefully in his mountain home
The trees are his beard, and the wind is his comb
    I see Grandfather Mountain

1993

The Price of Travel

It's expensive to travel these days, so why not just stay at home? I know I'm staying home more. I used to have to run all over town to do this and that: to go to the bank, to deliver articles to the paper, to go to the library, to go to a concert, to visit with friends. And now there's little need to waste this time and expense. I can do it all on the Internet. I can bank on the Internet, send articles to newspapers, visit the library, listen to a live concert, and email friends, all without having to get off my couch. I like the convenience, and I utilize it as much as possible. But I sometimes show up at the old places I used to visit without having any real reason to be there.

I sometimes show up in the new Shoppes in Farmer's Hardware, even though screwdrivers, wrenches, and saws have been replaced by arts and crafts. The ambiance of a seventy-five year old hardware store is still there: the nail bins, the saw wall, the nuts and bolts drawers, and the real wood counters and shelves. It's still a good place to wander around.

I like the access and organization provided by online banking, for someone such as myself who is not inclined to balance bank statements and who is inclined to lose receipts, it's a real asset. I guess we really don't need bills and coins much anymore, but I like having real money in my pocket and I still like to go to the bank.

I used to bring Mountainhome Music press releases to the *Mountain Times*, *Watauga Democrat*, and *Blowing Rocket*. But I don't need to do this anymore. I can type what I need, pull photos off the Internet or out of my picture files, and then press "send." What used to be a day's work is done in an instant. It's great. But many of the folks I used to know and call friends, well, I don't see them much anymore. And a newspaper office is a wondrously chaotic and creative place. I miss my visits there.

And now I can visit libraries all over the world and read articles and books on the Internet. But I occasionally visit the library anyway. It makes me feel smarter to walk among the corridors of books than to read what's on my computer screen.

You can hear a concert on the Internet, too. But I believe there's something special about being at a live performance that can't be recaptured. There's a synergy of time and place and emotion between audience and performers that is largely missing when music is squeezed through a thin wire.

Necessity is dictating that I drive less and work more. And I work as much as I can from the comfort of home. But sometimes I need go in old buildings, I need to be with busy people, I need to hold a dollar bill in my hand and turn the pages of a real book, I need to experience face-to-face conversation and spontaneity, and I need to play music with my friends. All of these things are virtually impossible on the Internet. Maybe three dollars a gallon isn't that bad.

2006

School Days

Elementary Wonder

In the second grade, I remember the Halloween Carnival at Bayview Elementary School. I remember the crowds, candy apples, and cotton candy. I remember a lot of adults wore big round buttons with a picture of a baldheaded man. The buttons said, "I like Ike." I didn't know who Ike was, but I remember I liked the "I like Ike" buttons and I wanted one. But I didn't get one.

I think the same year we were told we had to go up to the school one afternoon to get some medicine. Of course, I didn't want to go. I was thinking about the long needle that Dr. Temple used when he gave us shots. I didn't want the medicine. Besides, being sick wasn't always that bad. Sometimes, when I got better after being sick, which was usually a day or two, our family would eat out, and I was allowed to get a vanilla milkshake.

To get our medicine at school, we had to stand in a long line. When I came to the medicine table, I saw a nurse squirt something on to a sugar cube. No needle! I liked the medicine and wanted some more. It was a polio vaccine. The nurse said we could only have one medicine. I knew what polio was. A boy at my school had polio and had to wear leather and steel braces on his legs. I never saw the kid with polio play kickball.

One time when I was sick, though, I didn't get to stay at home. I had boils on my butt and mother made me take a pillow to school to sit on. Everyone looked at me. I felt like I was sitting on top of a tall mountain. It was terrible and made me sweat.

In the third grade I had to dress up like a little German boy for the Christmas pageant. Our class sang "O Christmas Tree," and we learned one verse in German. My costume was made of stiff leather shorts, and it had leather suspenders. I didn't like being a little German boy, but I did like "O Christmas Tree" with the German verse.

In the fourth grade for the May Day festival, our school had a flower contest. I had no interest in a flower contest. But then I heard that the winner got a silver dollar. I picked some flowers from my mother's garden and put them in a leftover Easter basket, and I took my flowers to school. The room where all the flowers were kept had big expensive arrangements, like they had been bought in a store. I felt ashamed. I wished I hadn't entered that silly contest. A day or two later they called my name and gave me the silver dollar. I still have it.

In the sixth grade I think I had my second real girl friend. I say *I think* because I'm not sure. It was near the end of the school year and we were playing kick ball. I think maybe I kicked a homerun or did something heroic and was feeling pretty proud. While I was resting under a pine tree, Donna came up and started talking to me. The prettiest girl in the school was talking to me! Then she started kicking my feet, just barely, not hard at all. I didn't understand why she was doing that. Then she stood on my left foot and a small sharp rock jabbed through my tennis shoe. I screamed in pain. She ran off, and we didn't get married.

The Inspiration of Lloyd

Lloyd Rhodes was somebody everybody in the 5th grade looked up to—and feared. He always wore tight blue jeans, a wide black leather belt, and a dirty white T-shirt. And he had a loud motorcycle at home. I heard it one time when I was delivering papers. It was loud and scary, just like Lloyd. I never saw him in a fight. I didn't need to. Everybody feared and respected Lloyd.

I wanted people to fear and respect me too, so one afternoon after school I chased down my good friend, Wayne. He didn't even know I was chasing him until I jumped and held him down on the ground and beat him in the face with both fists. He started crying, and I just kept punching: left, right, left, right, left, right, left, right. While I was punching, I realized that this wasn't the way it was supposed to be. He didn't fight back. How could I be thought of as tough if he didn't fight back? So I let him up. Still crying, he ran across the softball field back into the school. And I felt terrible. "If this is what's it like to be tough," I thought; "if this is what it's like to win a fight, then I don't want to be tough and I'll never fight again." And I never did, except with my brother.

1998

The Button

The thin metal strips had been wrapped around his teeth and implanted in his gums. Today, wires would be added, tightened and strung. As he was waiting for his name to be called, the music of the Drifters took him to a sunset on the beach, where a gentle breeze was blowing, where small waves were lapping on the shore, and where he was walking barefoot with his girlfriend under the boardwalk, just having some fun (sing) *under the boardwalk, boardwalk.*

She was his guest on this late afternoon picnic. Back at school she had cornered him in the hall and had given him a note to indicate her interest. He became nervous and started twisting a button on his new madras shirt. He twisted it clean off. "May I have that?" she asked.. "Now they were dating," he thought, "and soon they would be in love."

The trip to the beach was their first real date. Between hotdogs and cold slaw and beach volleyball, he kept his eyes on her. He was watching her to see if she was watching him. She was talking to the other girls and brushing back her windswept, strawberry hair.

As the summer sun sank into the Atlantic Ocean and the bright blue sky turned gray, she descended from a small grassy dune, and soon he found himself walking away from his Sunday School Class into the forbidden darkness with the most beautiful girl in the seventh grade.

To avoid a wave, she bumped into his side. To avoid a sharp seashell, she bumped into his side. Because it was getting dark and hard to see, she bumped into his side. He wondered why she couldn't walk straight.

When the gilding gulls and crescent moon were their only company, she pulled a snack-sized bag of chips from her shoulder bag and asked, "Would you like a chip?"

"Sure," he said, "sure," although he wasn't really hungry.

She put a chip halfway between her soft and salty lips, and she turned and tilted her head. A small wave tickled his feet and ran between his toes; he took a tiny step forward...and leaned...and stretched his neck. He took a nibble and then a bite and then another and then another and then another and then another. Waves washed over their souls as they ate a bag of BBQ chips with wrinkles. Her misty eyes were as deep as the ocean. ...He was hooked, and his heart was pounding.

"The doctor is ready to see you," called the nurse. As he stood up, he noticed he had been sitting next to a very pretty girl with freckles on her face and strawberry hair.

"This is your button," she said.

"But how? ... how?" he blushed slightly and picked it up; his fingers brushed across her soft, smooth skin.

"Ah, ah...do I know you?" he asked.

"Yes, my name is Megan, and I go to your school."

When his braces were tightened and it was time to go
    home,
Her chair was empty, for she had gone.
His mouth wasn't sore, and he felt no pain.
He kissed the button and whispered her name.

2004

Teacher Days

A Beginning Teacher

Will I fit in?
Will the children like me?
What if they don't listen, don't behave
And don't do their work?
Well, they should.
I know Bloom's Taxonomy,
Piaget's theory of cognitive development,
Skinner's behavior mod,
And Glasser's reality.
I know inclusion, exclusion,
Seclusion, and exhaustion.
I know math, science, and social studies,
Language arts, and literature,
Whole language, sign language,
And some Spanish.
But what if they still don't listen,
Still don't behave,
And still don't do their work?
What if they don't like me?
What if I don't fit in?
Why didn't they teach me this in college?

2000

The First Day of School

Mr. Murphy arrived at Mountainhome Middle School feeling slightly out of place. For twelve years his classroom had been many different classrooms all over North Carolina, wherein he had visited and taught and departed; his classroom had been teacher conferences and banquets and seminars; his classroom had been the highway and the hotels and movie screens; his classroom had been full of long, quiet spaces wherein he pondered problems of the world and the possibility of his return to full-time teaching.

Once the decision was made, he knew things would be different. He knew he would have to compromise the control of time and moments of joyful solitude. He was right.

On the first day, students filed into his classroom like the perfect kids in Wal-Mart newspaper ads: baggy pants on the boys, fresh haircuts, and new book bags covered with Blue Devils, Tarheels, Panthers, and Dale Earnhardt's #3. Some of the small girls wore little girl shirts and little girl shorts, and some of the larger girls wore little girl shirts and little girl shorts. Some of their faces were covered with sun-splashed freckles and some were splashed with unusual shades of brown and beige and red. For both boys and girls, there was an abundance of fresh enthusiasm for the new school year.

The first day began with introductions. There was Billy and Roger and Matthew—who wanted to be called Matt; and Sarah, Celia, and Suzanne, who wanted to be called Sue. Given the fourteen other names he had to learn and remember, Mr. Murphy decided to have the students create a name sign for their assigned seat. He passed out blank file-cards and colored markers, and he told his students to crease the card down the middle, write their names, and place the card on the front edge of their desks.

Matt wanted to know if he could use his own colored pencil. Celia wanted to know whether to fold the card long ways or short ways. Sarah wanted to know if she had to write in cursive. Billy said he could do it better on the computer. Roger wanted to know if he could draw a picture on his. Sue said her marker was dry and wanted to get a new one. Kaitlin said she didn't get a card, and Holly said she had a splinter in her hand and asked Mr. Murphy if he would pull it out. He looked at his watch, 8:30.

After the commotion had settled and names were shared, Mr. Murphy needed a student information card for his own file, so he gave the students another card. This time students were directed to write their name, address, phone number, and birthday. They were also told to write their parent or guardian's work number.

"Do you want my mom's cell and fax number?" asked Celia.

"Should I list my real dad, my stepdad, or my mom's boyfriend?" asked Billy.

"We just moved," said Roger, "and I don't know my new address yet."

Mr. Murphy looked at his watch, 8:45.

On the subject of birthdays, Scott wanted to know if he should round it off. He said, "I'm not really eleven. I'm eleven and two-thirds."

"But your birthday is still your birthday. Write down your birthday."

"But I'm eleven and two-thirds!" responded Scott.

"Write down your birthday. The day on which you were born," directed Mr. Murphy.

"Yes, sir."

Then everyone volunteered his or her age. Sarah called out, "I just had a birthday, and I'm eleven and two days." Sue said she was eleven and a half; Celia, eleven and two thirds; Jack, eleven and eleven twelfths. As this continued, Mr. Murphy thought about what a fine job last year's math teacher must have done teaching fractions.

Celia asked Mr. Murphy his age. Even though he was slightly self-conscious, he volunteered, "fifty-three."

"Whoa," responded Sarah.

"You're older than my PapPa, "said Billy.

"Are you married?" Sarah continued.

Mr. Murphy thought this was none of her business, but he wanted to be honest. "No," he answered.

Sarah quickly offered, "Do you want to date my granny? She's only thirty-five."

Mr. Murphy was saved by an announcement: it was now time for an orientation in the gym. Following the assembly, the students were scheduled to tour the school and to go to lunch with their exploratory teachers.

As the ocean calmed and the tide went out, Mr. Murphy reflected on his days of freedom and travel and solitude. "What have I gotten myself into?" he thought. "What have I gotten myself into?"

After a long teachers' meeting, he had an hour to spend before he could leave so he sat down to read and review an undiscovered novel. After turning a page or two of *Ulysses*, he noticed it was 3:30 and time to go home.

2004

Burnt Toast

Some of my colleagues complained about the smell of burnt toast in the teachers' lounge. This was soon after I decided that I'd eat my breakfast at school rather than at home. I am usually the first one in the building, so, along with my morning coffee and scan of the news on the Internet, I decided to enjoy a warm, crisp piece of jelly covered, wholegrain bread. There wasn't a toaster in the lounge, but it didn't matter. I had previous toasting experience in my microwave at home.

For my first piece of toast at school, I set the microwave at 45 seconds. My bread was warm but not too crisp. I covered it modestly with naturally sweetened grape jelly and, even though it wasn't perfect, it was a delightful contribution to my morning routine.

The next morning, I set the microwave at one minute, thinking that the additional 15 seconds would yield a crisper piece of bread. After a brief moment of personal relief, I returned to a smoke filled room. I quickly opened the windows and the door and watched the smoke pour into the empty hall. I feared the smoke alarms, and waited. The first bus pulled up and unloaded, and then another and another. No alarm.

Soon after other teachers began to arrive, I heard a voice in the hall, "Who burnt the bread?" I didn't volunteer a response and began work on my lesson plans.

To be safe, the next day I sat the microwave at 50 seconds, just five seconds longer than the first day. And for some reason, at about 35 seconds, silver gray smoke began to escape the door and a growing black hole began eating my bread. In need of some nutrition, I grabbed a honey bun from the vending machine and escaped down the hall.

I decided to try one more time. I sat the dial at 35 seconds and kept watch through the small, gray glass window. At about 30 seconds, I spotted smoke, popped open the door, and doused the hot spot with a spoon-full of grape jelly. I salvaged the outer crust. It wasn't much, but it was tasty.

I wondered, why would my toast be soft at 45 seconds one day and begin to burn at around 30 seconds on other days? Could it be the size of the bread or its thickness or its position on the spinning plate? Could it be variations in the dough or the humidity in the room? Or perhaps there was a series of serendipitous power surges at the Millers Creek Power Company? Could it be this or that? Perhaps? Perhaps?

On Thursday, Mrs. Blackburn confronted me about the irritations caused by my school-wide trail of smoke and smelly toast. Even though there was a rational explanation, I felt somewhat embarrassed as I began explain the variables of thickness and texture and humidity and power and how it was all beyond my control.

I left late on Thursday and, as always, arrived early the next morning. As I poured fresh water in the coffee maker, I noticed a brand-new toaster by the microwave—a gift, no doubt, from my considerate colleagues. I also noticed, on one end, a variety of light-to-dark settings: 1-2-3-4-5-6-7.

I cautiously moved the dial from 3 to 6, pushed the handle down, and waited. The thin wire strips creaked with heat. Heat waves began to rise. Drips of coffee reluctantly fell into the clear darkness. The invitation of warm bread filled the room.

I am pleased to say that I have almost achieved morning perfection: solitude, hot coffee, and properly textured toast. ...I like oatmeal for breakfast too, and have successfully made it in my microwave at home. It should work at school, shouldn't it? I'll let you know.

2005

Taking the Test

Students, give me your attention...I'm waiting. Good.

Notice your name and school number have been pre-marked on your answer sheet form. There are two number two pencils positioned in your pencil pouch and pointed to the left. Please raise your hand if you need pencils and the proctor will provide them for you. Okay, sit up straight. Open your Question Booklet and find question S-1. On your answer sheet form, find the corresponding S-1 located in the darkened space in the upper left hand corner.

Yes, what's your question? What does *corresponding* mean? I'm sorry. I'm not allowed to answer your question.

Now read question S-1. Next to answer S-1 on your answer sheet, you see four small bubbles. Fill-in bubble A, B, C, or D, the one that best represents the correct answer. When you fill-in the bubble, make sure the area you shade doesn't extend beyond the bubble's borders. If you break the bubble, the scoring device may detect an incorrect response and therefore record your answer as—wrong. So be careful. And remember, relax.

This test will take two hours. That is, you have two hours to take this test and if it takes you longer than that, too bad. Now some of you may finish early. If you finish early, take the time to review your responses, to clarify your bubbles, and to erase any stray marks. Stray marks may result in your responses being scored as—wrong. Make sure that for every question asked in the Question Booklet you have filled in the corresponding bubble on the Answer Sheet Form. Don't leave any bubble blank. If you're not sure of an answer, just guess.

The score you make on this test will determine whether or not you pass the eighth grade—and go to high school. Remember, relax. You may begin.

2002

The Last Day of School

I pay attention to the news. This week Iraq got an interim government, the president visited with the Pope, an angry man drove a bulldozer through Granby, Colorado, the economy and gas prices swung up, severe weather swept the nation, and, what had the greatest affect on me, this week, yesterday, was the last day of school for this school year.

The last few days were sort of amazing, particularly the last day. Teenagers who normally complain about having too much work were asking for more work.

"Can I wash the board?"

"I don't know if you can or not," I replied.

"May I wash the board?"

"You may."

Then a collage of voices rose up like smoke from burning leaves.

"May I empty the garbage?"

"May I take the posters off the wall?"

"Please do, and pull the tape off the back so the pictures won't stick together."

"May I, may I, may I? water the flowers, wipe the dust off the TV screen, sweep the floor, wash the desk tops, pull the tape gum off the walls, throw away the old newspapers, dust the bookshelves, wash the windows, empty my locker, throw away my science project, pull the thumb tacks out of the bulletin board, scrub the ink-spot off the floor..."

I didn't realize there was so much to be done. And even more, I didn't realize that they realized that there was so much that could be done. For much of the year I heard, "Why do we have to work so hard? Can we read a skinny book? Do we have to answer all the questions? Can we talk instead of work?"

Had the last day been any longer, we probably could have had the grass cut, had chipped bricks replaced, altered the landscape, and had a new roof put on the building. Somehow, I thought, I need to figure out how to spread this energy throughout the year.

When the work and the dust settled and anticipation for the final bell rose, some faces seemed to await the announcer's call, "Gentlemen, start your engines." Some faces were blank and some anxious, edging on tears. Without asking, some students wrote on the just cleaned board,

"I will miss you."

"Your homeroom was cool."

"You are the greatest."

One student placed an excessively stapled note in my hand that read, "Don't open this until after the bell rings."

When the bell rang and the ocean parted, and when the army of liberated eighth graders passed out of the doors of early adolescence, I opened and read the note in my hand.

"I didn't like you and I didn't like being in your class—for most of year, but I guess you're really okay. Sorry for the trouble I caused. I will miss you...you know who."

I stood in my classroom doorway, carefully removed all the staples from my note and placed it in my pocket. I looked across at my sparkling clean, empty room, turned and walked up the hall. I could hear the echo of each step, and I could recognize each of a thousand voices.

What a day.

2004

Short Tales

Just Tolerable

As far as we know, Grandpa was a potato famine refugee and the first American branch on the Shannon family tree. Soon after he arrived, he caught the gold rush fever and headed toward the western mountains of opportunity. How or exactly when he found his fortune isn't known, but somewhere near Carson City, Nevada the luck of this Irishman turned into a pot of gold. Given the fact that his teeth had rotted along with the Irish potato, and given his desire to savor the fruits of his good fortune, his first and largest investment was in a set of false teeth. Wanting something more stable than a whittler's work of art, and suspicious of the boom and bust banking system, he decided solid gold dentures would be both a stable and a secure investment. He commissioned a local blacksmith to design and refine, but as it turned out Grandpa's gums were slightly smaller than the hoofs of a plow horse. Unwilling to chisel down or reconfigure his investment, he decided to tolerate this mild discomfort.

Now we don't know how well the teeth worked or to what extent he kept them in. We do know that when Grandpa died, he willed his investment to his direct descendents, to the firstborn of future generations. Until last year, I was completely unaware that I was in line to possess a set of 150-year-old false teeth. Along with the dentures came Grandpa's last will and testament. In this partial history, he stipulated that they "shall not be remolded, melted, or sold." It also stated that he desired the teeth to remain in the family in perpetuity. "In perpetuity," now that stretches things out for a while. I guess Grandpa saw his gift as an opening to immortality.

Curious about their worth, a few months ago I took the teeth to America's yard sale, to the marketplace of antiquities. I had them appraised on the Millers Creek edition of Antiques Road Show. Here I learned that the blacksmith who created Grandpa's oral work of art had also designed an ornate golden gate for the first governor of California. And this gate apparently inspired the name for that famous arch that now stretches across the mouth of San Francisco Bay. I also learned that this arch, in turn, inspired a mid-western fast food entrepreneur to create his own set of golden arches. Given these associations, according to the appraisers, at auction, Grandpa's dentures would bring 50 to 60 times their actual value! Amidst my jubilance, I was quickly drilled by reality; that night I dreamed of Tantalus who couldn't get a drop of water, of a luxury liner that wouldn't float, of Marilyn Monroe whom I couldn't touch, of BBQ ribs that I couldn't eat, and of an ice-cold beer that I couldn't drink.

"Can't remold, can't melt, and can't sell." The words made me restless, and I started to scheme. I could insure the dentures for a large sum; then they could get lost or stolen, and then I would get a large settlement from the insurance company. But, of course, there was also the chance that I could get arrested and taken to jail. Or I could donate the dentures to some worthy cause and take a small bite from Uncle Sam's hand. But this would violate the "in perpetuity" clause and, when discovered, my branch on the Shannon family tree would likely be sawed-off, chopped-up, and ground into woodchips. This would be a big risk for a small gain.

"Can't remold, can't melt, and can't sell," There must be something I can do?

I'll tell you, a thin veneer of white enamel did no harm, and thanks to gum pads and Poly-grip, Grandpa's investment is stable, secure, and tolerable, just tolerable.

2006

Travelers' Tech

Traveler: I was traveling this Thanksgiving, like I am on most Thanksgivings. My mother and my home place are in Orange Park, Florida, just outside of Jacksonville. This year, every year, that is my Thanksgiving destination. Since gas is still high and advanced airline tickets are relatively low, I flew home this year.

The Charlotte airport was crowded, as I knew it would be, but I moved out of long-term parking, into the terminal, through e-ticket confirmation, and past baggage check without too much trouble.

Just before passing through the metal detector, I informed the attendant of my titanium shoulder. On signal, as always, I was pulled aside and inspected by a magic wand and a light frisk. Given all the luggage and laptops and shoes and bodies and body parts that these folks have to thoroughly inspect, and given that most folks are in a hurry to catch a flight and a cup of Starbucks, I was very impressed by my inspector's easygoing manner.

Inspector: Please sit down, raise your right foot, your left foot; please stand up, raise your right arm, your left arm.

Traveler: My right arm won't go up.

Inspector: Yes, sir. I see.

Traveler: The magic wand confirms.

Inspector: That's okay...

Traveler: ...he says, and he continues his work. He pats my right arm, my left arm, my right leg, my left leg.

Inspector: You're done. Thank you for your cooperation.

Traveler: Thank you, I respond. I was proud to have done my part for homeland security. Then I gathered my book and belt, coins and keys, glasses and pens, shoes and satchel, and I'm on my way.

Comfortable with a cup of warm coffee and a pecan-covered Cinnabon, I savor the security of being at my designated gate with time to spare. The waiting area was lightly sprinkled with travelers, and I go to what seems to be the least congested, quietest corner. No sooner had I taken a sip, a bite, and turned a page or two of my book, my silence was shattered.

(Airport chatter in the background)

Lady on cell phone: Yea, I'm at the Charlotte airport, waiting on my flight, there's a light rain, but it's not too bad...put your father on the phone...I love you, too. George, make sure you get the soup on....yes, yes, I know...how many...what...where'd they come from?....

(Lady continues her conversation while announcer speaks)

Announcer: Your attention please. Your attention please. Passengers awaiting flight 791 to Jacksonville, please move to boarding area C-11.

Lady on cell phone: ...put two in the den...fold down the couch...wait a minute, wait a minute I thought they said something about my flight....Guess not...next year we'll have to draw the line...was it natural or a C-section?...she had so much trouble...and that sorry husband of hers...I don't care if he is your brother.

Announcer: Passengers awaiting flight 791 to Jacksonville, please move to boarding area C-11. Due to mechanical difficulties, we are putting you on a different plane.

Lady on cell phone: ...Turn the stereo down, it's hard to hear...I said it's hard to hear...It's hard to hear! Yes, I said it's just a light rain...I didn't need my umbrella...I paid Reba $50.00. It better hold a curl or I'll demand a refund...Yes, six cans of soup...look behind the baked beans...not the lima beans, the baked beans, the baked beans...the bright red can with beans on the front! Everybody's moving...I better go...I better go...I better go...I love you too....

Traveler: I moved with the crowd to waiting area, C-11. I quickly noticed that one kid was watching a DVD of *Animal Planet* and one, *Old Yeller*—I was waiting for my plane, waiting for peace and quite, and waiting to arrive at my destination. I found some solace in another cup of coffee, another bite of my Cinnabon, and another chapter. After a few sips, bites, and paragraphs, I remembered that I had a cell phone.

(Airport chatter gets louder, a roaring lion and a bellowing elephant are in the background.)

(dialing) 1-903-269-4021. Carla, this is Joe, I'm still in Charlotte...a little rain...it's like a zoo here. You haven't left yet, good...well, I'm gonna be about an hour late...yea, coming in would be better than circling around...I know you don't mind...well, thanks for bringing her...Right, high tech's not her thing...Okay, thanks again. Bye.

(Airport noise fades out)

The flight home went well. My experience reminded me that there is no refuge, no escape from the curses and conveniences of modern technology.

By the way, this show is being recorded for your future listening enjoyment.

2006

I Am

Work is Never Done

Work is a place to have my name on a mailbox or a door or a seat or chair or place in line; my place to tighten the bolt, steer the wheel, answer the phone, change a tire, hoist a sail, file the mail, or surf the web; my place to sell products and skill, wisdom and worthiness; my place to sell or to share with others.

Work is what I *have* to do earn a living, and what may I *choose* to do extent my talents. It's an obligation and an opportunity, compliance and conformity, connection and self-expression.

I am a plumber and electrician, a teacher and musician, a preacher and politician. I am a business owner and entrepreneur, a parent and child, a Civitan and everyman.

I labor for my children and my children's children, for community and country. I labor for the present and the future, for my beliefs and my ideals.

I labor for the temporal and the essential, for the passing and the eternal.

My work is never done.

2006

A Single Voice

When ministers speak of God,
When shamans speak of Vision,
When poets speak of Truth,
When lovers speak of Love,
If I hear a single voice,
I hear them all the same.

When teachers speak of Knowledge,
When writers speak of Inspiration,
When musicians speak of Harmony,
When dancers speak of Balance,
If I hear a single voice,
I hear them all the same.

When the fearful speak of Safety,
When the weary speak of Rest,
When the oppressed speak of Justice,
When the enslaved speak of Freedom,
If I hear a single voice,
I hear them all the same.

1995

Closer

I am sometimes jealous.
I sometimes hate.
I am sometimes resentful.
Sometimes it feels good to carry a grudge.
Some people I don't like.
Some neighbors I don't love.
Depending on how she looks, I may covet my
    neighbor's wife.
I sometimes take the Lord's name in vain.
I have doubts.

But I believe
When I acknowledge my doubts, I am closer to faith.
When I acknowledge what I do not know, I am closer
    to knowing.
When I acknowledge my inadequacies, I am closer to
    being whole.
When I acknowledge what I am not, I am closer to
    "I Am."

2001

Country Roads
Less Traveled

Bill Monroe

Bill Monroe is widely referred to as the Father of
Bluegrass. Some may wonder what he did to achieve this
recognition. Some may not distinguish bluegrass from
country or folk music and therefore wonder: What is
bluegrass? Others may question why any of this matters. I
will very briefly try to answer these questions.

Bill Monroe was born on September 13, 1911 in
Rosine, Kentucky. He was the youngest of eight children,
and, as might be expected, he was surrounded by music. His
mother was a ballad singer and multi-instrumentalist. His
father was a renowned flatfoot dancer, and many of his
siblings were also fine instrumentalists. Bill wanted to play
too, but that meant being included. He didn't feel included
— in addition to being the youngest, he had a cross-eye,
which brought teasing and ridicule. He became shy and
withdrawn. When he was finally allowed to play music with
his brothers, he was told to play the mandolin, since it was
small and didn't make much noise. While still a young boy,
his parents died, and Bill moved in with his uncle, Pendleton
Van Driver. The personal and musical bonds were strong,
and soon Bill was accompanying fiddling Uncle Pen at shows
and dances. Young Bill was also attracted to the sounds of
local black bluesman, Arnold Shultz. Because of Shultz's
influence, the blues found its way into Bill's mandolin.

When the Depression hit, work that paid a living
wage was hard to find in eastern Kentucky, and, like many
southern boys, Bill went north seeking a livable and reliable
income. He found employment at an oil refinery in
Chicago, where brothers Charlie and Birch already worked.

The Monroe boys *had* to work, but music was their
passion. Opportunity came first as dancers on the WLS Barn

Dance, which required weekend work on the road. Soon it was discovered that the Monroes could also play and sing. As more opportunities came their way, they had to decide: quit the day job and go for it as musicians or keep the day job and continue to play part-time. Birch decided to stay off the road; somebody had to have a reliable income to pay the bills and to have a little money to send back home. Charlie was offered a job singing on KFNF in Shenandoah, Iowa, but he didn't want to do it alone. He invited Bill to join him. In 1933, music became a full-time job for Charlie and Bill Monroe.

They traveled from town to town, radio station to radio station; they developed their own style and repertoire and a significant following. One follower, in particular, confronted Bill with a surprise. While performing in Charlotte, North Carolina, a young woman Bill had spent some time with in Iowa showed up and told him that she was pregnant with his child. Bill Monroe married Carolyn Minnie Brown on October 18th 1936 in Spartanburg, South Carolina. As Bill entered into a new relationship, his relationship with Charlie began to fray. They had different ideas about their music—and also about the need for a manager. Charlie thought they needed a manager to help expand their opportunities. Bill thought this would mean giving up artistic control—and he wouldn't even consider it. Their brotherly fabric tore apart in 1938, and so, too, did their shared musical journey.

Bill started searching for his own sound. He moved to Little Rock and formed a band; this was short-lived, and he then moved on to Birmingham to try again. And again, it wasn't right. Maybe a duo was his sound? He ran an ad for a partner in the Atlanta Constitution. A young man named Cleo Davis responded, auditioned, and was hired. It was a good match—too good. They sounded too much like the old Monroe Brothers, and, to Bill, this was unacceptable. He had to have his own sound. So he experimented with a variety of instruments. He toyed with tempos and pitch and harmonies. He began to like what he heard, and he settled on a name—Bill Monroe and His Bluegrass Boys. And it didn't take them long to reach for the top. They traveled to Nashville and auditioned for the grand old judge of the Grand Ole Opry, George Hay. After hearing "Foggy Mountain Top," "Mule Skinner Blues," and "Fire on the Mountain," the Judge told Bill, "...if you ever leave here, you'll have to fire yourself." Their first performance was on October 28, 1939.

Thanks to WSM and the Grand Ole Opry, Bill Monroe and his music found a wide and loyal audience. Records were made, concerts were sold out, and money rolled in, mostly cash. Bill didn't trust banks. Times were good, for a while, but life on the road was lonely. Even though he was a man of deep tradition and propriety, fidelity was a weakness. In many towns and many places, Bill sought and found companionship. The pattern was so pronounced; it was no secret. Even Carolyn knew. Family dissension found its way into the band. Bill, often aloof, cold, and distant, became even more so, but his music remained magic. Seemingly, the tension in his personal life found expression in song, but the tension in the band was less than creative, even destructive. The Bluegrass Boys became a swinging door with well-worn hinges for those entering and exiting the employment of Bill Monroe.

Bill's first banjo player, Dave Akeman (a.k.a., Stringbean) turned his attention to full-time comedy in 1945, so Bill needed someone else to fill this role. Fiddler Jim Shumate, who had joined Bill two years earlier, told him about a banjo player named Earl Scruggs. When singer and guitar player Lester Flatt found out that there might be a new banjo player, his response was, "this Scruggs fellow can leave his banjo in its case." He thought the group sounded better without a banjo. However, once Flatt heard Scruggs play, he advised Bill, "Hire him no matter what it costs."

When Earl Scruggs and Lester Flatt became a part of the Bluegrass Boys, it seems that Bill Monroe finally found his sound: In addition to his mandolin, he had Earl's smooth, syncopated, hard driving three finger-style banjo; he had Lester's steady rhythm guitar and welcoming voice, he had Chubby Wise's versatile fiddle (replaced Jim Shumate), and Howard Watts' (a.k.a. Cedric Rainwater) steady bass (replaced Howdy Forrester).

He didn't know it yet, but bluegrass was becoming more than his band's name. It was becoming a style, a genre of American music. Flatt and Scruggs played a major part. With Flatt and Scruggs, Bill Monroe and his Bluegrass Boys performed and recorded from 1946 to 1948. Partly because of dissension and largely because Earl figured he could make more money with his own band, in February of 1948 Earl Scruggs left Bill Monroe. Lester Flatt followed about two weeks later. Lester Flatt and Earl Scruggs formed the Foggy Mountain Boys soon thereafter—and they maintained Monroe's sound. Bluegrass was expanding.

But Bill Monroe was possessive. He thought bluegrass music was *his* music. He became angry at anyone who copied *his* sound. This included not only Flatt and Scruggs, but also the Stanley Brothers. Perhaps because Bill helped put their name on the map, and because they had been Bluegrass Boys, he directed most of his rage at Flatt and Scruggs. They were playing *his* music—and they were becoming rich and famous in the process.

The arrival of Elvis and early rock and roll almost decimated bluegrass music. Rock and roll pushed it off the airwaves and out of the concert halls. But Flatt and Scruggs prospered with the theme for the Beverly Hillbillies, "The

Ballad of Jed Clampett," with "Foggy Mountain Breakdown" and other hits. Other bluegrass musicians didn't fare as well, including Bill Monroe. Hard times were ahead.

On January 20, 1953 Bill was in a head-on collision that almost took his life. He recovered, but given the musical currents of the time, staying alive financially was a struggle. In 1957 he barely broke even; in 1958 he ran a deficit and his car was repossessed; and in 1959, again, he barely broke even. To add to his misery, Carolyn filed for divorce, which the court granted on August 12, 1960. To say the least, Bill needed help.

Somewhat ironically, this help came from a cultural outsider: a Jewish, New Jersey-based scholar and folklorist named Ralph Rinzler. Rinzler, a musician himself, respected Bill's music and appreciated its quality, its integrity, and its place in the narrative of traditional American music. To make a long story short, Rinzler, who had also discovered Doc Watson, became Bill's manager, popularized the phrase, "The Father of Bluegrass," and wrote about Bill in national publications. Like he did with Doc Watson—he integrated Bill into the 1960s nationwide folk music boom. Bill needed help. He didn't ask for it; his pride would not allow it. But once given, it was appreciated and it made a profound difference in one man's life and one nation's musical heritage.

The Stanleys, once Bill's competition, became his friends. And on some occasions either Carter or Ralph would sit in with the Bluegrass Boys. When Carter Stanley died, Bill placed his hand on his casket and said, "We will meet again." In February 1980, Bill collapsed; the diagnosis was colon cancer. He thought he had played his last note. Shortly before being taken into surgery, there was a knock on the door of his hospital room. Earl Scruggs slowly walked in and the two men shook hands. Earl thanked Bill for putting the banjo in bluegrass and for saving him from life as a millworker. Bill recovered from the surgery—and rediscovered an old friend.

For his contributions to the arts world, Bill Monroe was inducted into the Country Music Hall of Fame in October 1970; he was awarded the "Lifetime Achievement Award" by the National Association of Recording Arts and Sciences in 1993 and the National Medal of the Arts on October 5th, 1995. Obviously, Bill Monroe achieved legendary status long before his death on September 9th, 1996. Today there is bluegrass music in Russia, Japan, throughout Europe, and indeed all around the world.

To return to the questions I asked as I began this story. How did Bill Monroe achieve recognition? If you didn't already know, hopefully you know more now. What is bluegrass? In my opinion, it is the sound that comes the closest to the sound of his 1946-48 Bluegrass Boys. Why does it matter? Why do we turn on the radio in the car? Why do we plant flowers? Why do we stand on mountaintops and gaze at the view? I don't know why it matters, I only know it does.

2005

References

Smith, Richard, D. Can't You Hear Me Calling: The Life of Bill Monroe, Little Brown and Company, New York, 2000.

Rosenberg, Neil, V. Bluegrass: A History, University of Illinois Press, Chicago, 1993.

The Man in Black

From 1969 to 1971 I religiously watched the *Johnny Cash Show* on ABC. After the opening announcements, he would turn and announce, "Hello, I'm Johnny Cash." I listened to the man in black.

From 1969 to 1971 my wings were still wet as I faced the storms of Vietnam, political assassinations, volatile race relations, and changing American and personal values. I had more questions than answers, but at that time I could not acknowledge this, not even to myself. Johnny Cash gave voice to my voice: he sang songs about prisoners and preachers, about the homeless and helpless, about soldiers and seekers; he was angry and articulate, passionate, and proud. I listened to the man in black.

I listened to his story about growing up in Dyess, Arkansas, picking cotton and listening to his sister sing hymns to lighten the load. I listened to his story about a native American who helped to raise the flag at Iwo Jima, who became a reluctant hero, who drank too much and died in two inches of water in an Arizona ditch. I listened to his story about a teenaged boy who fell in love with the beautiful girl next door. She moved to Hollywood and become a star, but the glitter didn't glow, and she gave it all up to return to the boy next door who worked at the candy store.

I listened to the story about the just released prisoner whose life would not last long enough to make it home, so he tells a stranger, "Give my love to Rose please, won't you mister. Take her all my money, tell her to buy some pretty clothes, and tell my boy that daddy's so proud of him, and don't forget to give my love to Rose."

I listened to his anger in "Folsom Prison Blues," his fatalism in "I Guess Things Happen that Way," his longing in "I Still Miss Someone," his hope in "Man in Black," and his faith in "These Hands."

In more recent years he couldn't get his records played by an industry he helped to create. Beholden to no one, he sat alone in front of a microphone and sang and played his reflections on life. These reflections were often played on public radio, and I listened to the man in black. And so did many others. For this effort he won the 1995 Grammy Award for Contemporary Folk Album of the Year.

From his first number one hit, "I Walk the Line," in 1956; to his 2003 MTV Video of the Year award called "Hurt"—the music, the songs, and the stories of Johnny Cash defied a category and an establishment. In fact, he seemed to stubbornly resist being defined by others in any way, perhaps because of a greater need to define himself. And he did so, continuously. And I listened to the man in black.

It was said of Johnny Cash, "he a poet, he's a picker, he's a prophet, he's a pusher; he's a pilgrim and a preacher and a problem when he's stoned; he's a walking contradiction, partly truth and partly fiction, takin' every wrong direction on his lonely way back home." *(Kris Kristofferson, The Pilgrim, Chapter 33.)*

All along the way he sang and shared his journey. His voice became the voice of the downtrodden and disadvantaged and the sinner and the seeker; his voice became the voice of generations and a nation. And all along the way, I listened to the Man in Black.

The Old Gospel Ship

Puberty hit at about the same time that Elvis and Pat Boone were vying for our nation's soul. I was encouraged to avoid Elvis and to emulate Pat Boone, which is why I wore white buck shoes and secretly listened to "All Shook Up." I liked Pat Boone *and* Elvis. By the age of twelve, I had lost my innocence.

Uncle Earnest lost his innocence too. As a young man, he had been a model of propriety: a popular high school athlete, always neatly dressed and groomed, well respected in the community. As an older man, he was somewhat less concerned with propriety. His clothes were often wrinkled and dirty; his shoes untied. He constantly kept a stubble beard, and he kept the stub of a cigar in his mouth, which he used to chew on, not to smoke.

As an older man, he also started playing music, country music. He played what he called his Hawaiian guitar (a steel guitar). He would say to me, "Joe Wayne, let's go back here and let me play you a song. Back here was in the back room at my grandmother's house in Valdosta, Georgia, a place full of wonderful music. But Uncle Earnest's music wasn't fully appreciated. He knew that, and so did I. But I felt proud to be invited to listen, and I listened closely. "Now this is a Carter Family song," he'd say, and he played "The Wildwood Flower." And then he would sing one, always the same one. "Now this is a Carter Family song," he'd say, "The Old Gospel Ship."

> *I'm going to take a trip on the old gospel ship,*
> *I'm going beyond the skies.*
> *I'm going to shout and sing until the bells do ring*
> *Until I bid this world good-bye.*

93

I'd sit and listen and was very impressed, not so much by his playing and singing, but by the fact that he could sing without his cigar falling out of his mouth. Since I was visiting, I would spend the night. He always went home, across town, across the tracks, out of sight and out of mind.

Breakfast at my grandmother's house always included a bowl of Shredded Wheat and freshly baked biscuits that were soft enough for a thumb in the side and sturdy enough to hold a chunk of butter and a large dose of maple syrup. And thanks to an old, cream-colored Philco radio, we always had famous guests at the table: Hank Snow, Eddie Arnold, Patsy Cline, Earnest Tubb, and many others. I enjoyed their company.

I didn't listen to country music at home, and I can't honestly say what I liked the most: Elvis or Earnest Tubb, Pat Boone or Patsy Cline, "Wings of a Dove" or "Bye Bye Love." I liked it all. Uncle Earnest was more particular. He listened to and played country music. In his world, that's all there was and all he cared about.

Apparently, his concern for social conventions diminished after the war, after a horrific night in a Middle Eastern desert, after he woke up one morning and discovered that most of the men in his platoon would never wake again. Whatever that does to a man, it was done.

When he came home, he aspired to work as a laborer on South Georgia roads; he became a social outcast, a lonely bachelor, and a barebones musician. It seems, the more he struggled, the more important music became. He played wherever he could, for whomever would listen. But mostly he played at home, mostly for himself.

Perhaps the last verse of "The Gospel Ship" spoke to his sense of loneliness and difference:

> *If you are ashamed of me, you ought not to be.*
> *And you better have a care.*
> *If too much fault you find, you'll sure be left behind*
> *While I'm sailing through the air.*

He knew it well when others found fault. No doubt, he desired acceptance, but not as conventionally available. He needed more than a clean shave, more than clean clothes and more than social approval. He needed more. Perhaps in some measure, music filled these sacred spaces. I think it did. I hope so.

When he died in 1992, I was given his Hawaiian guitar. Today, from inside its dusty black case, it makes more memories than music—memories of war, of innocence lost, and of music and its power to heal. Like Uncle Earnest and like millions of others, I make music too. I have to. I must.

1998